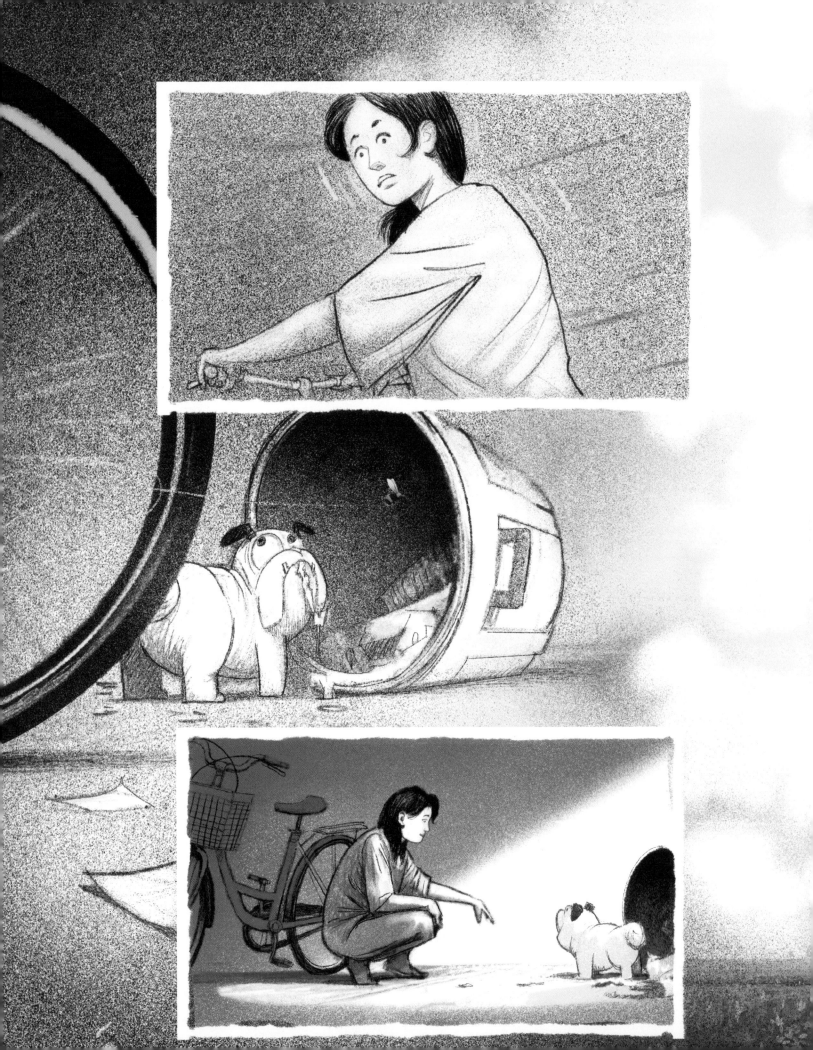

SumoPuppy

DAVID BIEDRZYCKI

Charlesbridge

To Benjamin Jace and Calvin James

A special thank you to Jason Harris and the students of Eisugakkan High School in Fukuyama, Japan

Copyright © 2022 by David Biedrzycki
All rights reserved, including the right of reproduction in whole or in part in any form.
Charlesbridge and colophon are registered trademarks of Charlesbridge Publishing, Inc.

At the time of publication, all URLs printed in this book were accurate and active.
Charlesbridge and the author are not responsible for the content or accessibility of any website.

Published by Charlesbridge
9 Galen Street
Watertown, MA 02472
(617) 926-0329 • www.charlesbridge.com

Library of Congress Cataloging-in-Publication Data
Names: Biedrzycki, David, author, illustrator.
Title: SumoPuppy / written and illustrated by David Biedrzycki.
Description: Watertown, MA: Charlesbridge, [2022] | Audience: Ages 5–8. | Audience: Grades K–1. |
   Summary: When puppy Chanko-chan is adopted by a sumo heya, she is eager to learn how to be
   her best self among the wrestlers, but unfortunately she gets off to a slow start with SumoKitty.
Identifiers: LCCN 2021031426 (print) | LCCN 2021031427 (ebook) | ISBN 9781623543013 (hardcover)
   | ISBN 9781632899408 (ebook)
Subjects: CYAC: Cats–Fiction. | Dogs–Fiction. | Sumo–Fiction. | Wrestling–Fiction.
Classification: LCC PZ7.B4745 Sug 2022 (print) | LCC PZ7.B4745 (ebook) | DDC [E]–dc23
LC record available at https://lccn.loc.gov/2021031426
LC ebook record available at https://lccn.loc.gov/2021031427

Printed in China
(hc) 10 9 8 7 6 5 4 3 2 1

Illustrations done in pencil, watercolor, and digital kitchen sink
Display and text type set in Cafeteria by Tobias Frere-Jones
Printed by 1010 Printing International Limited in Huizhou,
   Guangdong, China
Production supervision by Mira Kennedy
Designed by Diane M. Earley

It is said that a bumblebee's body is too big and its wings are too small for it to fly.

But the bumblebee doesn't know that, so it flies anyway.

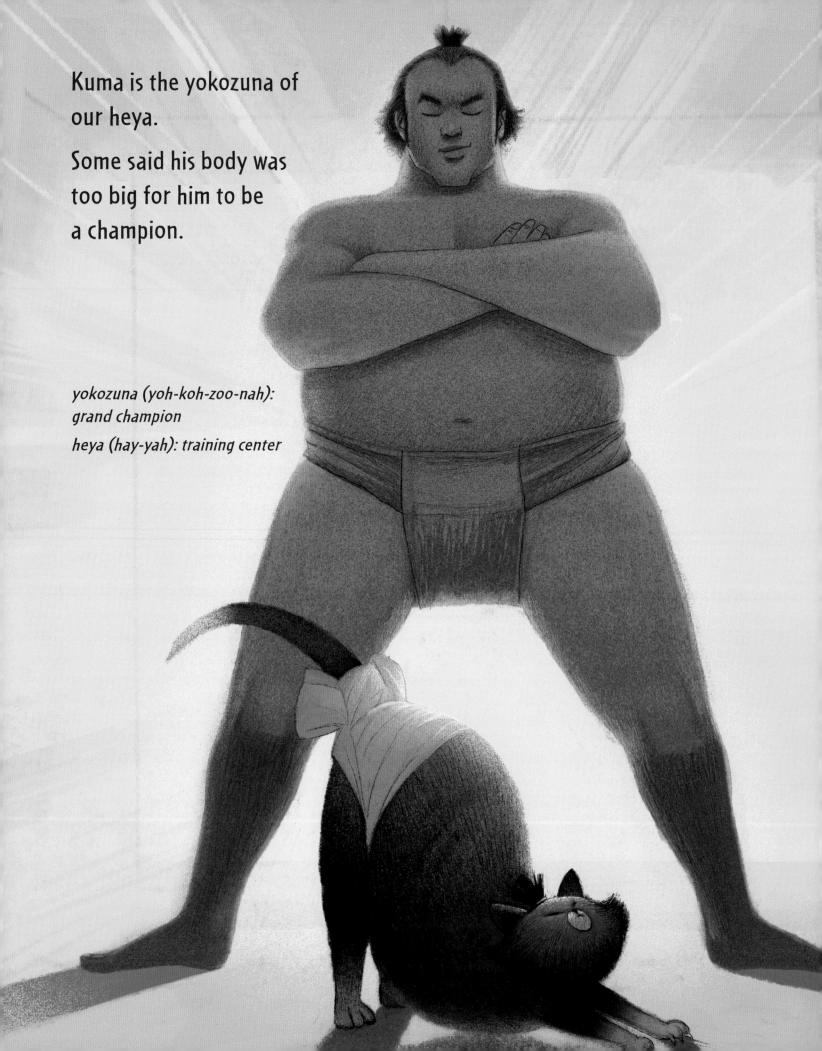

Kuma is the yokozuna of our heya.

Some said his body was too big for him to be a champion.

yokozuna (yoh-koh-zoo-nah): grand champion
heya (hay-yah): training center

But he didn't know that.
Now he is the best of the best.
I am his friend, SumoKitty.

Kuma is older and wiser now.

He no longer wishes to battle in the dohyō.

dohyō (doh-hyoh): ring

Instead he teaches others the wisdom he has learned.

I have grown older, too. I wish to catnap more and chase mice less.

I want to pass on my wisdom, but there are no kitties nearby to teach. They all live on the other side of the river.

Everything changed the day Okamisan brought home . . .

a puppy!

The rikishi named her Chanko-chan. It didn't bother me that everyone wanted to play with her.

okamisan (oh-kah-mee-sahn):
manager of the heya

rikishi (ree-kee-shee):
wrestlers

It bothered me that she wanted to play with me.

Only me.

She followed me everywhere.

Everywhere!
I couldn't get away.

During the day she blocked the sun where I slept.

WOOF!

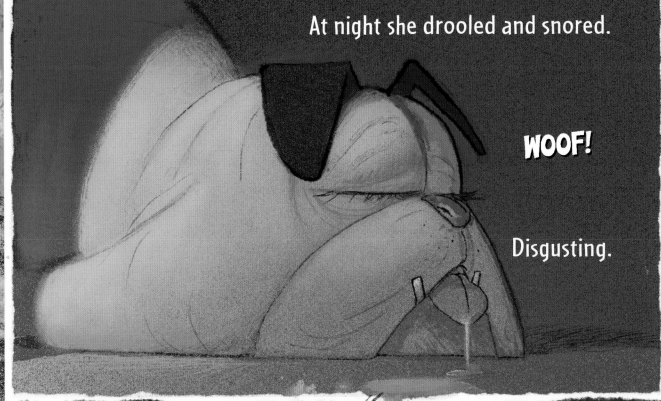

At night she drooled and snored.

WOOF!

Disgusting.

I couldn't do my job with
Chanko-chan around.

It was frustrating.

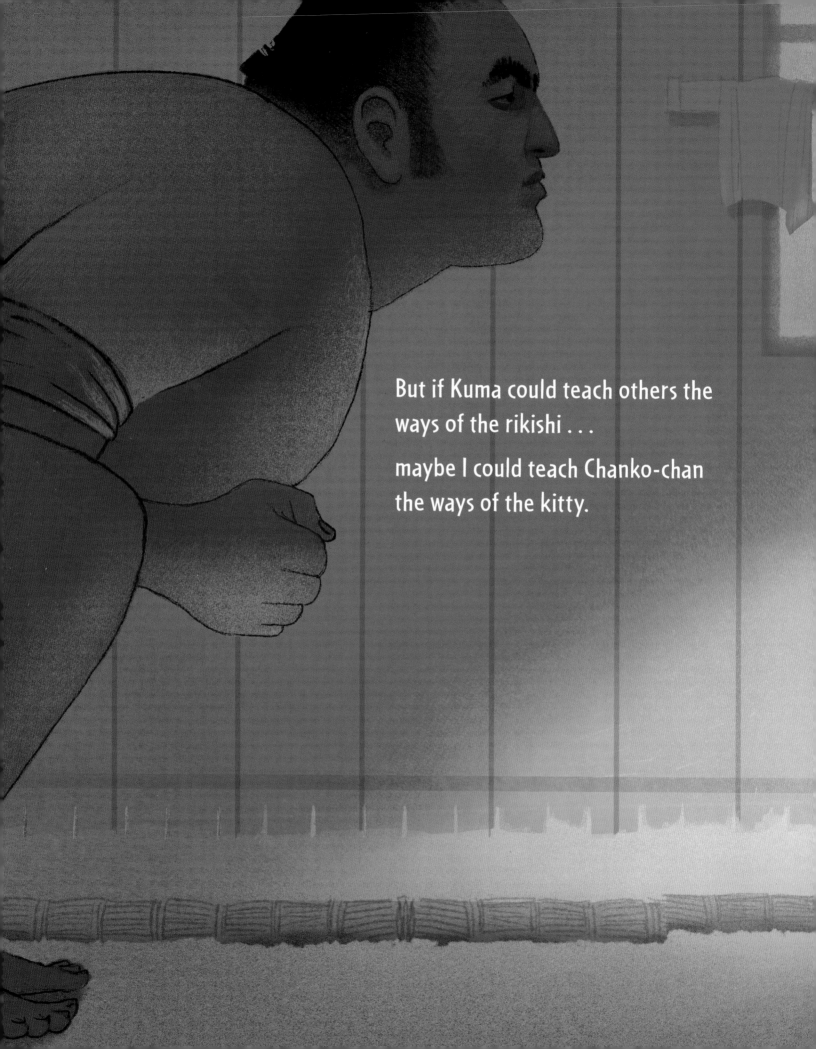

But if Kuma could teach others the ways of the rikishi . . .

maybe I could teach Chanko-chan the ways of the kitty.

She seemed eager to learn.

WOOF!

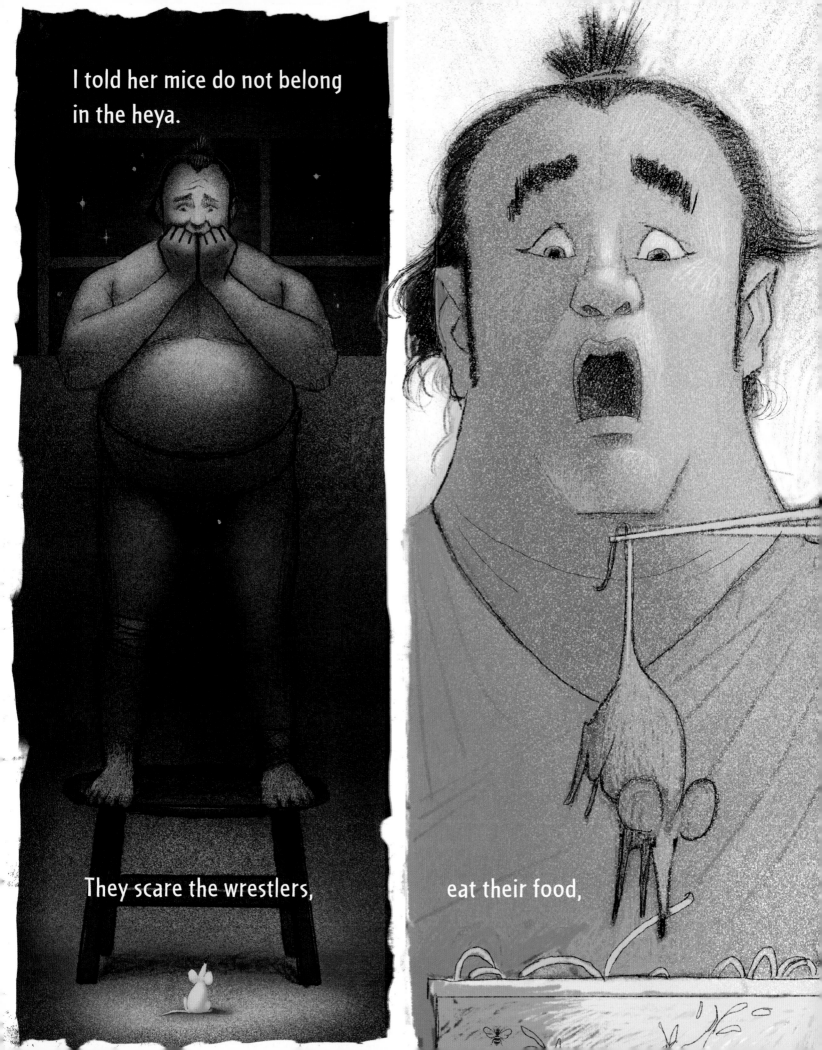

I told her mice do not belong in the heya.

They scare the wrestlers,

eat their food,

cause fires,

and poop all over.

To catch a mouse, you must first learn to act like a kitty.

Kitties do not fetch.

They are happy
to see no one.

They do not eat everything.

And they do not bring home underwear.

WOOF!

To hunt like a kitty,
be alert.

Spot your prey.

Slowly climb into position.

Get ready to pounce.

Do not pass gas.

Chanko-chan just didn't seem to get it. The only thing she was good at was barking.

WOOF! WOOF!

She barked at everything.

WOOF! WOOF!

Even herself.

WOOF!

One night it got so annoying the rikishi put her outside.

I went out and sat with her.
I told her I had a hard time
in the beginning, too.

The mice laughed at me.
I lost my job. But I didn't
give up. I had to find my place.

Chanko-chan didn't want to give up, either.
The next night she quietly stood guard over the heya.

When she heard something scamper across the floor . . .

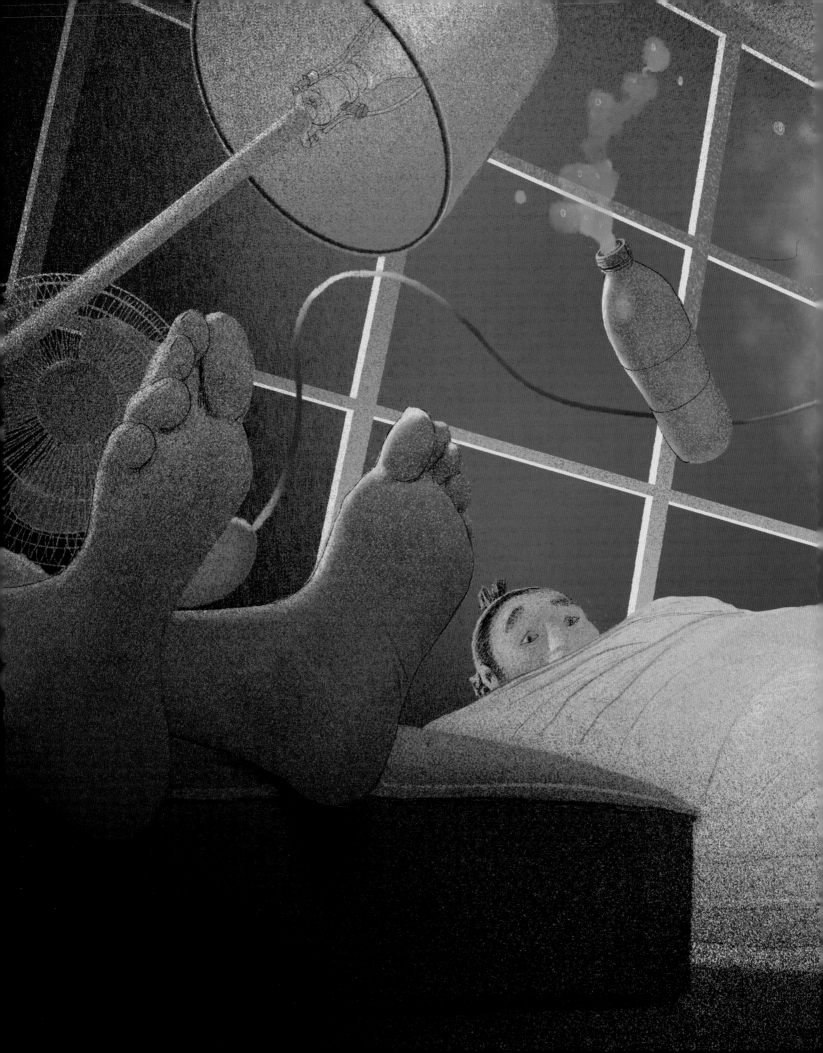

Even though she captured the mouse, no one was pleased.

Okamisan decided the heya
was no place for a puppy.

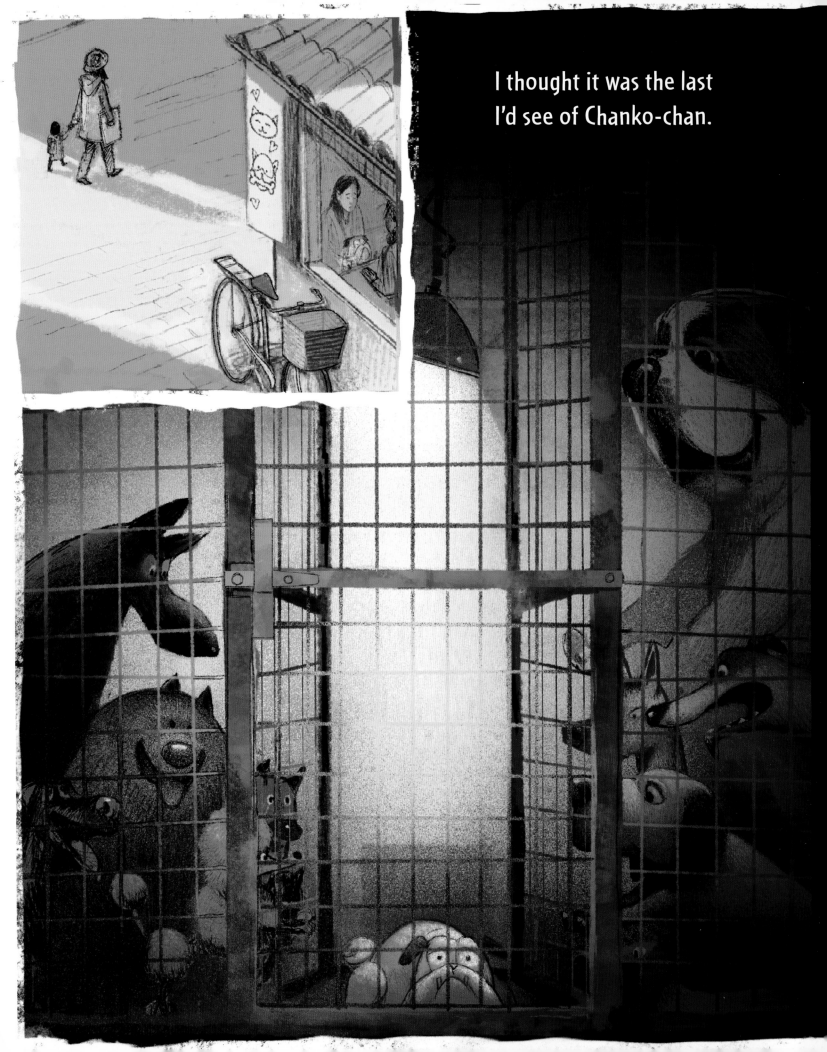

I thought it was the last I'd see of Chanko-chan.

But she had other plans.

It is said that dogs have a way of
finding the people who need them.

Early one morning Chanko-chan
returned to find us in danger.

WOOF!

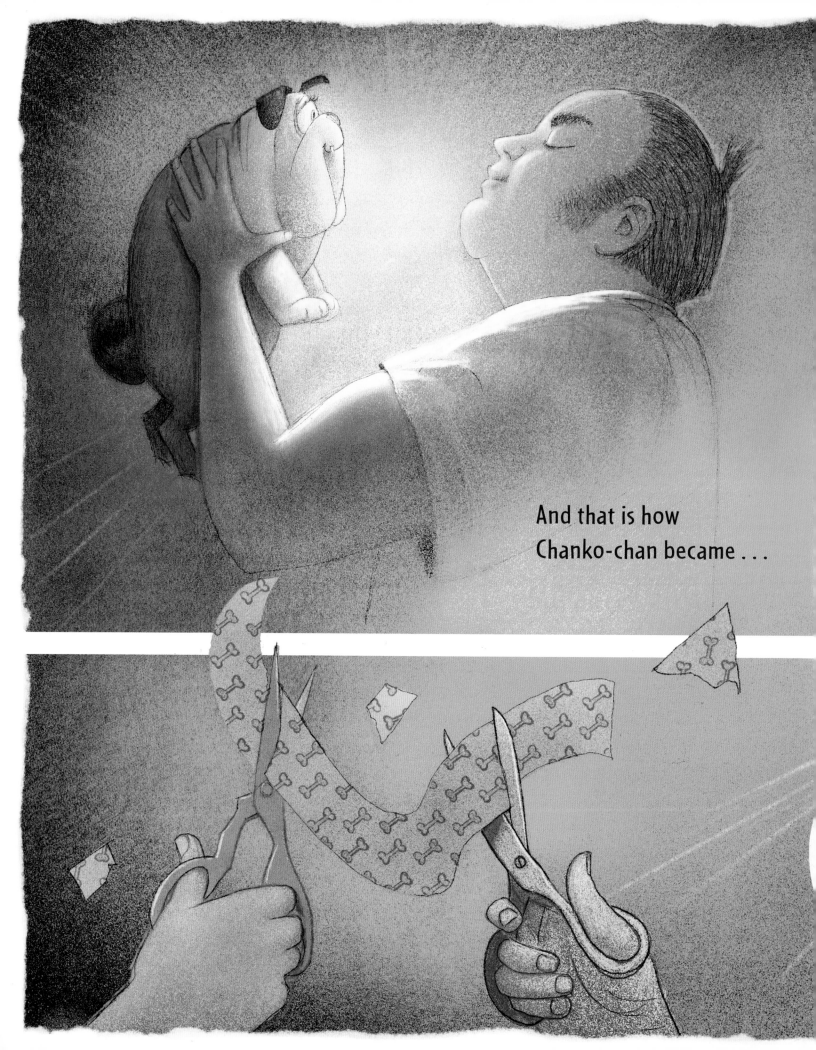

And that is how
Chanko-chan became . . .

SumoPuppy!

Some say a dog's body is too big
and it has no wings to fly.

Chanko-chan doesn't know that.

She flies anyway!

WOOF!